Dr. Seuss™

A CLASSIC TREASURY

Dr. Seuss: A Classic Treasury

This omnibus edition first published in the United Kingdom in hardback in 2004
by HarperCollins Children's Books.
This edition first published in 2008 by HarperCollins Children's Books.
HarperCollins Children's Books is a division of HarperCollins Publishers,
1 London Bridge Street, London SE1 9GF

Visit our website: www.harpercollins.co.uk

10 9

ISBN: 978-0-00-728882-3

www.harpercollins.co.uk

Printed and bound by Printing Express, Hong Kong

Dr. Seuss™

A CLASSIC TREASURY

HarperCollins *Children's Books*

THE CAT IN THE HAT

The sun did not shine.
It was too wet to play.
So we sat in the house
All that cold, cold, wet day.

I sat there with Sally.
We sat there, we two.
And I said, "How I wish
We had something to do!"

Too wet to go out
And too cold to play ball.
So we sat in the house.
We did nothing at all.

So all we could do was to

Sit!

Sit!

Sit!

Sit!

And we did not like it.

Not one little bit.

And then
Something went BUMP!
How that bump made us jump!

We looked!

Then we saw him step in on the mat!

We looked!

And we saw him!

The Cat in the Hat!

And he said to us,

"Why do you sit there like that?"

"I know it is wet
And the sun is not sunny.
But we can have
Lots of good fun that is funny!"

"I know some good games we could play,"
Said the cat.
"I know some new tricks,"
Said the Cat in the Hat.
"A lot of good tricks.
I will show them to you.
Your mother
Will not mind at all if I do."

Then Sally and I
Did not know what to say.
Our mother was out of the house
For the day.

But our fish said, "No! No!
Make that cat go away!
Tell that Cat in the Hat
You do NOT want to play.
He should not be here.
He should not be about.
He should not be here
When your mother is out!"

"Now! Now! Have no fear.
Have no fear!" said the cat.
"My tricks are not bad,"
Said the Cat in the Hat.
"Why, we can have
Lots of good fun, if you wish,
With a game that I call
Up-up-up with a fish!"

“Put me down!” said the fish.
“This is no fun at all!
Put me down!” said the fish.
“I do NOT wish to fall!”

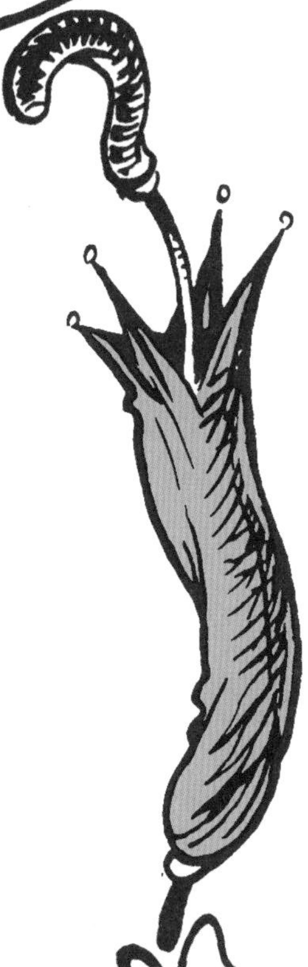

“Have no fear!” said the cat.
“I will not let you fall.
I will hold you up high
As I stand on a ball.
With a book on one hand!
And a cup on my hat!
But that is not ALL I can do!”
Said the cat . . .

“Look at me!
Look at me now!” said the cat.
“With a cup and a cake
On the top of my hat!
I can hold up TWO books!
I can hold up the fish!
And a little toy ship!
And some milk on a dish!
And look!
I can hop up and down on the ball!
But that is not all!
Oh, no.
That is not all . . .

"Look at me!
Look at me!
Look at me NOW!
It is fun to have fun
But you have to know how.
I can hold up the cup
And the milk and the cake!
I can hold up these books!
And the fish on a rake!
I can hold the toy ship
And a little toy man!
And look! With my tail
I can hold a red fan!
I can fan with the fan
As I hop on the ball!
But that is not all.
Oh, no.
That is not all. . . ."

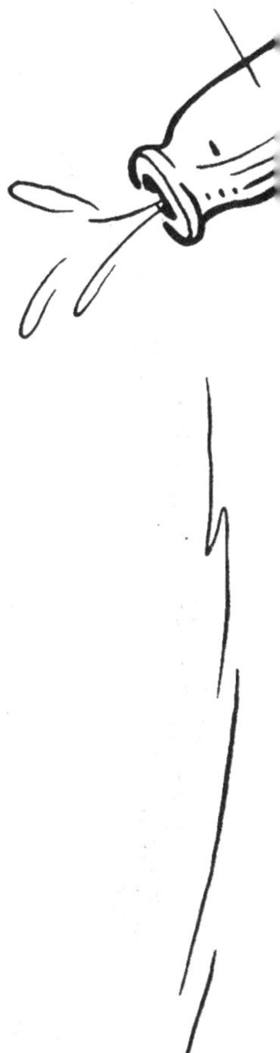

That is what the cat said . . .
Then he fell on his head!
He came down with a bump
From up there on the ball.
And Sally and I,
We saw ALL the things fall!

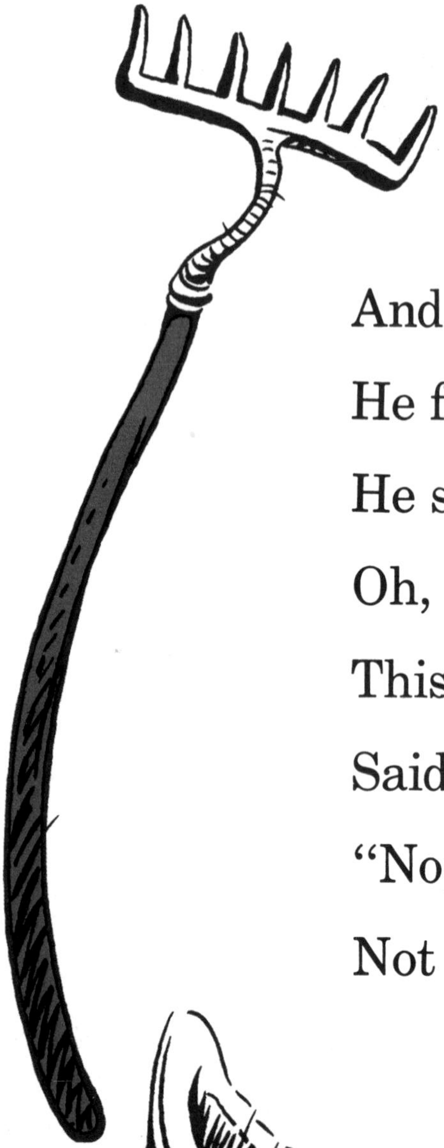

And our fish came down, too.
He fell into a pot!
He said, "Do I like this?
Oh, no! I do not.
This is not a good game,"
Said our fish as he lit.
"No, I do not like it,
Not one little bit!"

"Now look what you did!"
Said the fish to the cat.
"Now look at this house!
Look at this! Look at that!
You sank our toy ship,
Sank it deep in the cake.
You shook up our house
And you bent our new rake
You SHOULD NOT be here
When our mother is not.
You get out of this house!"
Said the fish in the pot.

"But I like to be here.
Oh, I like it a lot!"
Said the Cat in the Hat
To the fish in the pot.
"I will NOT go away.
I do NOT wish to go!
And so," said the Cat in the Hat,
"So

so

so . . .

I will show you
Another good game that I know!"

And then he ran out.
And, then, fast as a fox,
The Cat in the Hat
Came back in with a box.

A big red wood box.

It was shut with a hook.

"Now look at this trick,"

Said the cat.

"Take a look!"

Then he got up on top
With a tip of his hat.
"I call this game FUN-IN-A-BOX,"
Said the cat.
"In this box are two things
I will show to you now.
You will like these two things,"
Said the cat with a bow.

"I will pick up the hook.
You will see something new.
Two things. And I call them
Thing One and Thing Two.
These Things will not bite you.
They want to have fun."
Then, out of the box
Came Thing Two and Thing One!
And they ran to us fast.
They said, "How do you do?
Would you like to shake hands
With Thing One and Thing Two?"

And Sally and I
Did not know what to do.
So we had to shake hands
With Thing One and Thing Two.
We shook their two hands.
But our fish said, "No! No!
Those Things should not be
In this house! Make them go!

"They should not be here
When your mother is not!
Put them out! Put them out!"
Said the fish in the pot.

"Have no fear, little fish,"
Said the Cat in the Hat.
"These Things are good Things."
And he gave them a pat.
"They are tame. Oh, so tame!
They have come here to play.
They will give you some fun
On this wet, wet, wet day."

"Now, here is a game that they like,"
Said the cat.
"They like to fly kites,"
Said the Cat in the Hat.

"No! Not in the house!"
Said the fish in the pot.
"They should not fly kites
In a house! They should not.
Oh, the things they will bump!
Oh, the things they will hit!
Oh, I do not like it!
Not one little bit!"

Then Sally and I
Saw them run down the hall.
We saw those two Things
Bump their kites on the wall!
Bump! Thump! Thump! Bump!
Down the wall in the hall.

THIN
1

Thing Two and Thing One!
They ran up! They ran down!
On the string of one kite
We saw Mother's new gown!
Her gown with the dots
That are pink, white and red.
Then we saw one kite bump
On the head of her bed!

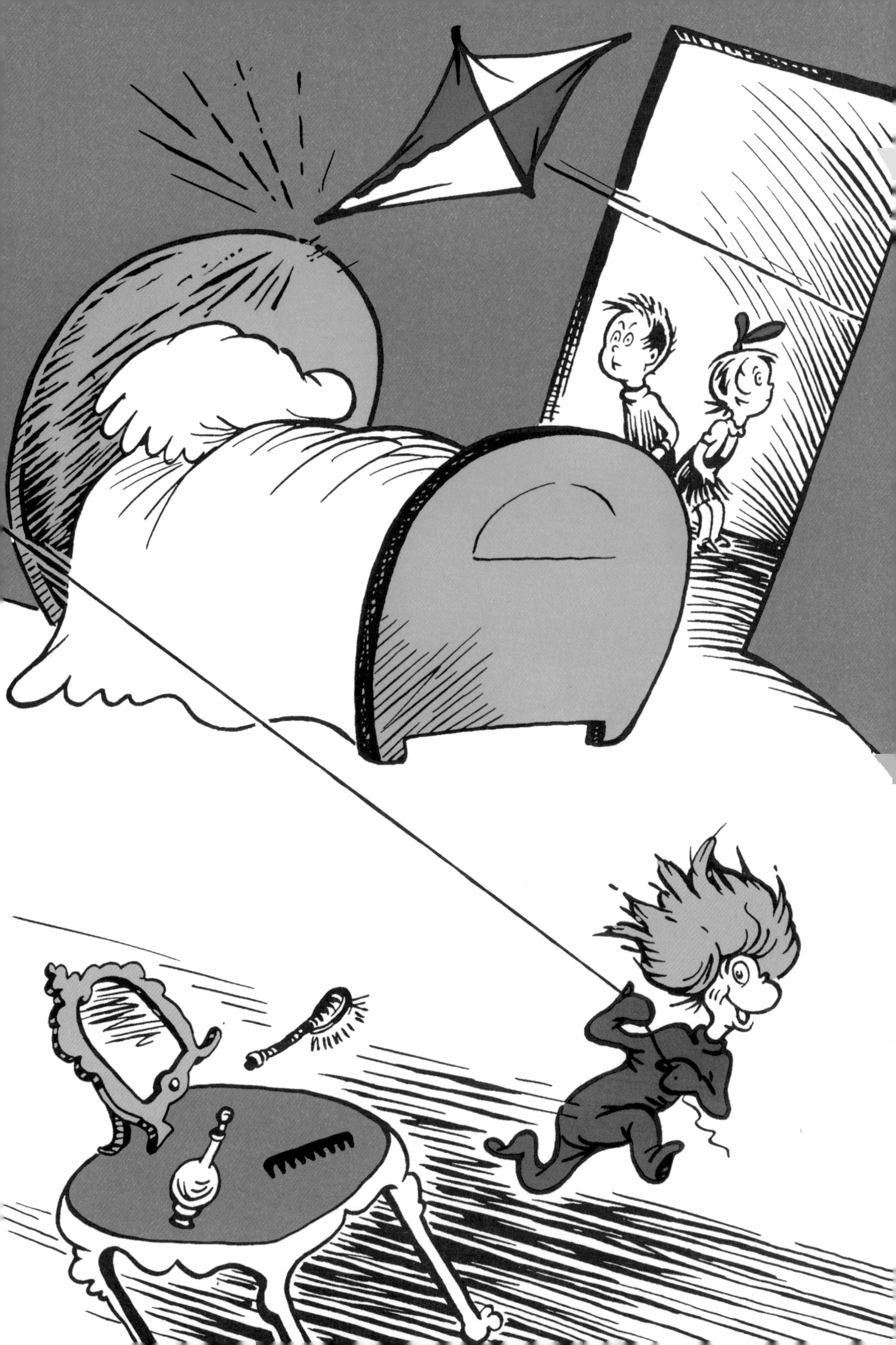

Then those Things ran about
With big bumps, jumps and kicks
And with hops and big thumps
And all kinds of bad tricks.
And I said,
"I do NOT like the way that they play!
If Mother could see this,
Oh, what would she say!"

Then our fish said, "LOOK! LOOK!"
And our fish shook with fear.
"Your mother is on her way home!
Do you hear?
Oh, what will she do to us?
What will she say?
Oh, she will not like it
To find us this way!"

"So, DO something! Fast!" said the fish.

"Do you hear!

I saw her. Your mother!

Your mother is near!

So, as fast as you can,

Think of something to do!

You will have to get rid of

Thing One and Thing Two!"

So, as fast as I could,

I went after my net.

And I said, "With my net

I can get them I bet.

I bet, with my net,

I can get those Things yet!"

Then I let down my net.
It came down with a PLOP!
And I had them! At last!
Those two Things had to stop.
Then I said to the cat,
"Now you do as I say.
You pack up those Things
And you take them away!"

“Oh dear!” said the cat.

“You did not like our game . . .

Oh dear.

What a shame!

What a shame!

What a shame!”

Then he shut up the Things
In the box with the hook.
And the cat went away
With a sad kind of look.

"That is good," said the fish.
"He has gone away. Yes.
But your mother will come.
She will find this big mess!
And this mess is so big
And so deep and so tall,
We can not pick it up.
There is no way at all!"

And THEN!

Who was back in the house?

Why, the cat!

“Have no fear of this mess,”

Said the Cat in the Hat.

“I always pick up all my playthings

And so . . .

I will show you another

Good trick that I know!”

Then we saw him pick up
All the things that were down.
He picked up the cake,
And the rake, and the gown,
And the milk, and the strings,
And the books, and the dish,
And the fan, and the cup,
And the ship, and the fish.
And he put them away.
Then he said, "That is that."
And then he was gone
With a tip of his hat.

Then our mother came in
And she said to us two,
"Did you have any fun?
Tell me. What did you do?"

And Sally and I did not know
What to say.
Should we tell her
The things that went on there that day?

Should we tell her about it?

Now, what SHOULD we do?

Well . . .

What would YOU do

If your mother asked YOU?

THE CAT IN THE HAT COMES BACK!

This was no time for play.
This was no time for fun.
This was no time for games.
There was work to be done.

All that deep,
Deep, deep snow,
All that snow had to go.

When our mother went
Down to the town for the day,
She said, "Somebody has to
Clean all this away.
Somebody, SOMEBODY
Has to, you see."
Then she picked out two Somebodies.
Sally and me.

Well . . .

There we were.

We were working like that

And then who should come up

But the CAT IN THE HAT!

“Oh-oh!” Sally said.
“Don’t you talk to that cat.
That cat is a bad one,
That Cat in the Hat.
He plays lots of bad tricks.
Don’t you let him come near.
You know what he did
The last time he was here.”

"Play tricks?" laughed the cat.
"Oh, my my! No, no, no!
I just want to go in
To get out of the snow.
Keep your mind on your work.
You just stay there, you two.
I will go in the house
And find something to do."

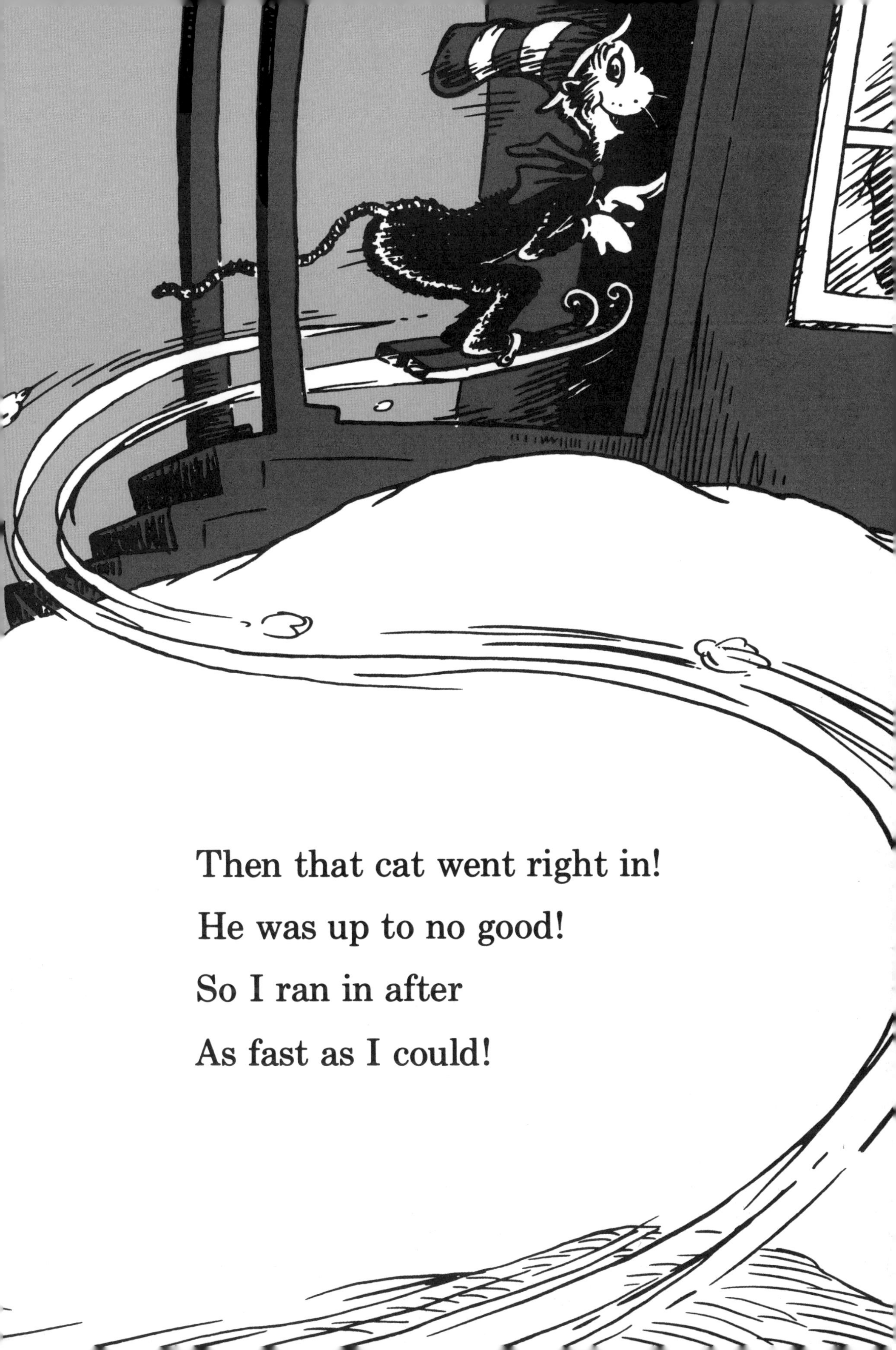

Then that cat went right in!
He was up to no good!
So I ran in after
As fast as I could!

Do you know where I found him?
You know where he was?
He was eating a cake in the tub!
Yes he was!
The hot water was on
And the cold water, too.
And I said to the cat,
"What a bad thing to do!"

"But I like to eat cake
In a tub," laughed the cat.
"You should try it some time,"
Laughed the cat as he sat.

And then I got mad.
This was no time for fun.
I said, "Cat! You get out!
There is work to be done.
I have no time for tricks.
I must go back and dig.
I can't have you in here
Eating cake like a pig!
You get out of this house!
We don't want you about!"
Then I shut off the water
And let it run out.

The water ran out.
And then I SAW THE RING!
A ring in the tub!
And, oh boy! What a thing!
A big long pink cat ring!
It looked like pink ink!
And I said, "Will this ever
Come off? I don't think!"

"Have no fear of that ring,"
Laughed the Cat in the Hat.
"Why, I can take cat rings
Off tubs. Just like that!"

Do you know how he did it?
WITH MOTHER'S WHITE DRESS!
Now the tub was all clean,
But her dress was a mess!

Then Sally looked in.
Sally saw the dress, too!
And Sally and I
Did not know what to do.
We should work in the snow.
But that dress! What a spot!
"It may never come off!"
Sally said. "It may not!"

But the cat laughed, “Ho! Ho!
I can make the spot go.
The way I take spots off a dress
Is just so!”

“See here!” laughed the cat.
“It is not hard at all.
The thing that takes spots
Off a dress is a wall!”
Then we saw the cat wipe
The spot off the dress.
Now the dress was all clean.
But the wall! What a mess!

"Oh, wall spots!" he laughed.
"Let me tell you some news.
To take spots off a wall,
All I need is two shoes!"

Whose shoes did he use?
I looked and saw whose!
And I said to the cat,
"This is very bad news.
Now the spot is all over
DAD'S £7 SHOES!"

"But your dad will not
Know about that,"
Said the cat.
"He will never find out,"
Laughed the Cat in the Hat.
"His £7 shoes will have
No spots at all.
I will rub them right off
On this rug in the hall."

"But now we have rug spots!"
I yelled. "What a day!
Rug spots! What next?
Can you take THEM away?"

“Don’t ask me,” he laughed.
“Why, you know that I can!”
Then he picked up the rug
And away the cat ran.

"I can clean up these rug spots
Before you count three!
No spots are too hard
For a Hat Cat like me!"

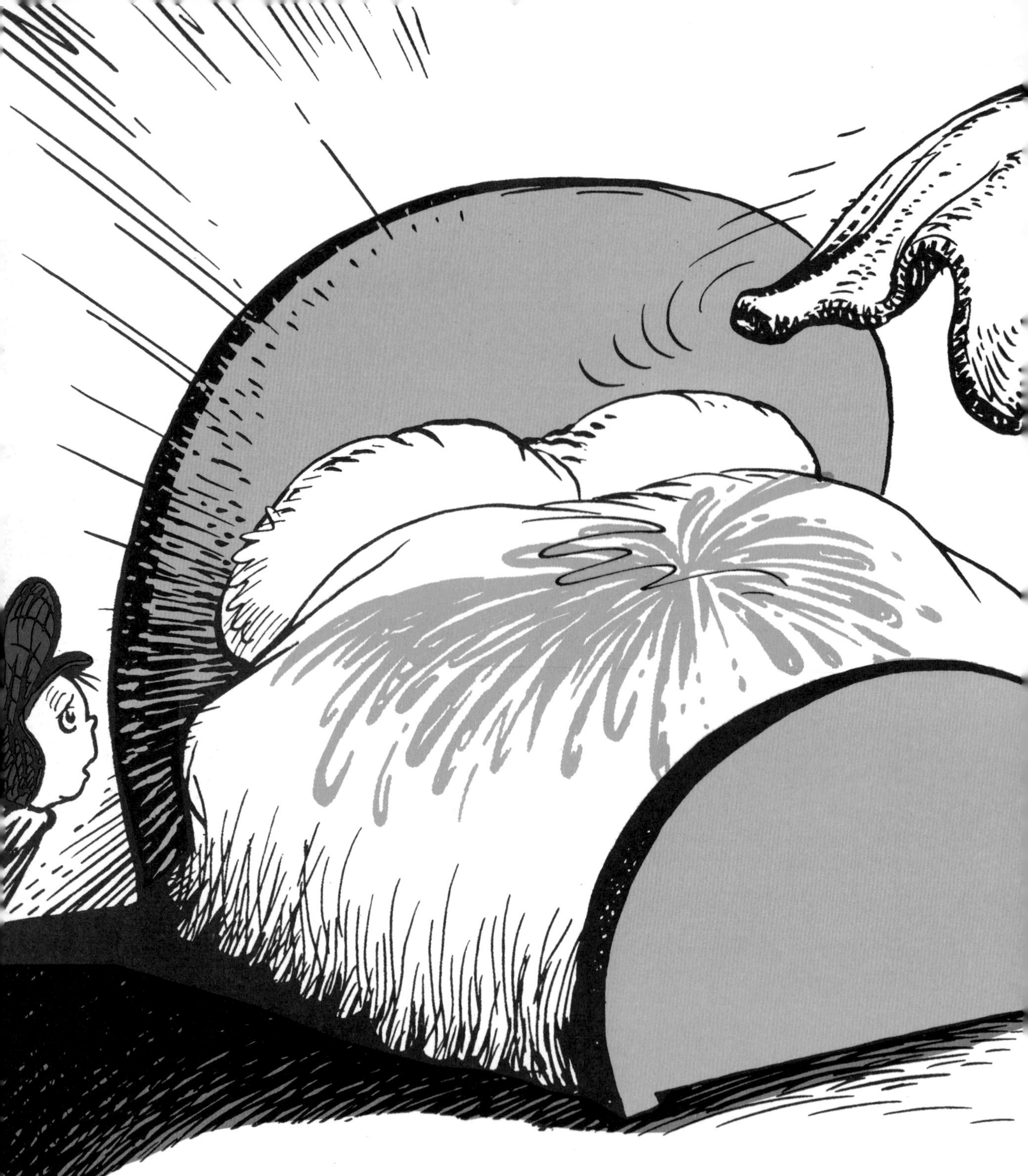

He ran into Dad's bedroom
And then the cat said,
"It is good that your dad
Has the right kind of bed."

Then he shook the rug!

CRACK!

Now the bed had the spot!

And all I could say was,

"Now what, Cat?

NOW what?"

But the cat just stood still.
He just looked at the bed.
"This is NOT the right kind of a bed,"
The cat said.
"To take spots off THIS bed
Will be hard," said the cat.
"I can't do it alone,"
Said the Cat in the Hat.

"It is good I have some one
To help me," he said.
"Right here in my hat
On the top of my head!
It is good that I have him
Here with me today.
He helps me a lot.
This is Little Cat A."

A

And then Little Cat A
Took the hat off HIS head.
"It is good I have some one
To help ME," he said.
"This is Little Cat B.
And I keep him about,
And when I need help
Then I let him come out."

B
A

And then B said,
"I think we need Little Cat C.
That spot is too much
For the A cat and me.
But now, have no fear!
We will clean it away!
The three of us! Little Cats B, C and A!"

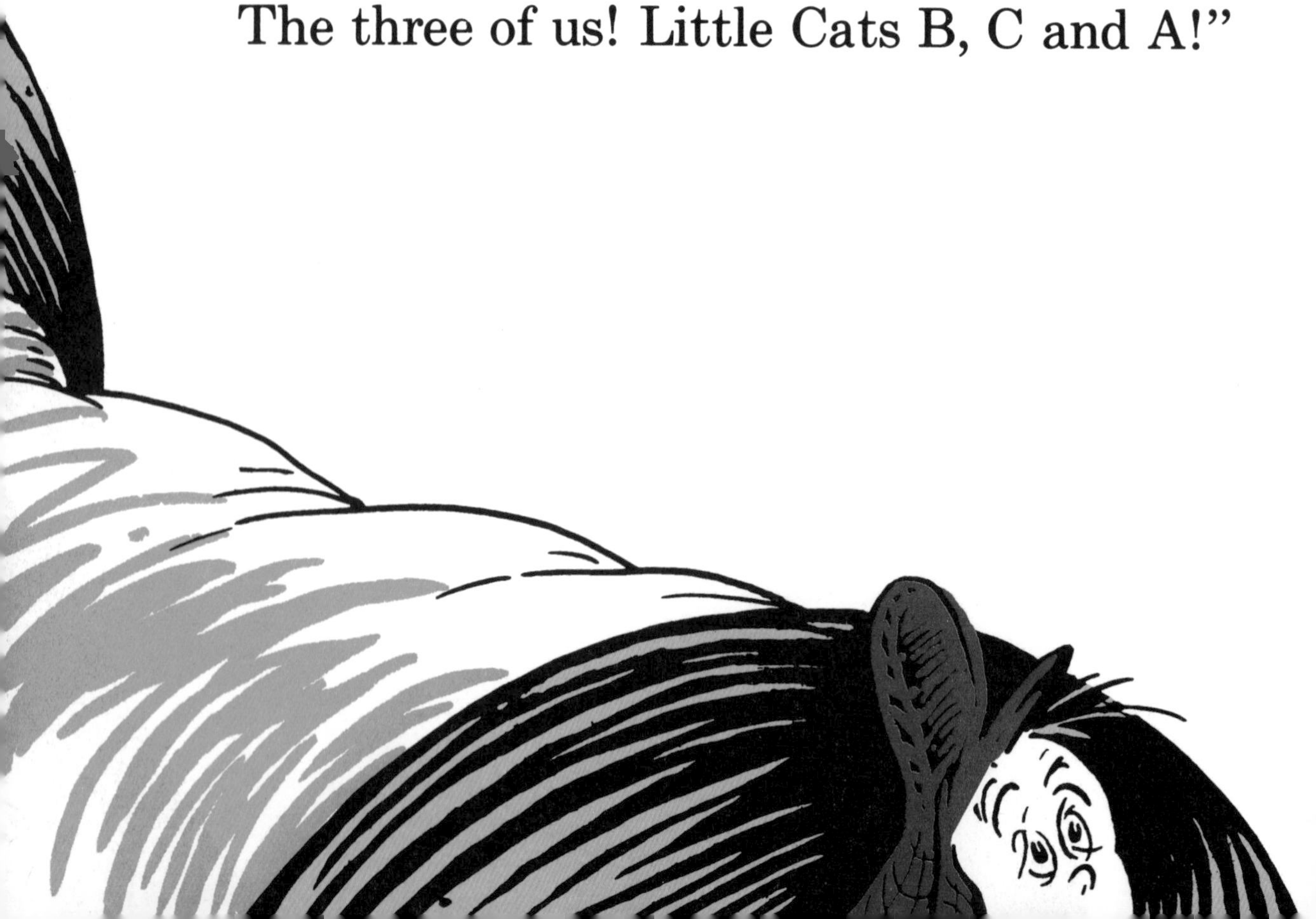

C
B
A

"Come on! Take it away!"
Yelled Little Cat A.

"I will hit that old spot
With this broom! Do you see?
It comes off the old bed!
It goes on the T.V."

And then Little Cat B
Cleaned up the T.V.

He cleaned it with milk,
Put the spot in a pan!
And then C blew it out
Of the house with a fan!

“But look where it went!”

I said. “Look where it blew!

You blew the mess

Out of the house. That is true.

But now you made Snow Spots!

You can’t let THEM stay!”

“Let us think about that now,”

Said C, B and A.

“With some help, we can do it!”
Said Little Cat C.
Then POP! On his head
We saw Little Cat D!
Then, POP! POP! POP!
Little Cats E, F and G!

"We will clean up that snow
If it takes us all day!
If it takes us all night,
We will clean it away!"
Said Little Cats G, F, E, D, C, B, A.

They ran out of the house then
And we ran out, too.
And the Big Cat laughed,
"Now you will see something new!
My cats are all clever.
My cats are good shots.
My cats have good guns.
They will kill all those spots!"

But this did not look
Very clever to me.
Kill snow spots with pop guns?
That just could not be!

“All this does is make **MORE** spots!”
We yelled at the cat.
“Your cats are no good.
Put them back in your hat.

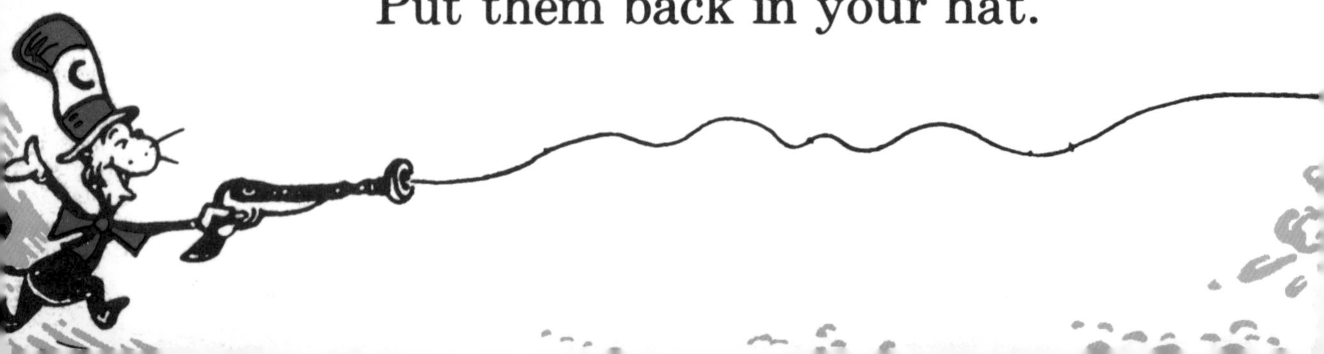

"Take your Little Cats G,
F, E, D, C, B, A.
Put them back in your hat
And you take them away!"

"Oh, no!" said the cat.
"All they need is more help.
Help is all that they need.
So keep still and don't yelp."

Then Little Cat G
Took the hat off his head.
"I have Little Cat H
Here to help us," he said.

"Little Cats H, I, J,
K, L and M.
But our work is so hard
We must have more than them.
We need Little Cat N.
We need O. We need P.
We need Little Cats Q, R, S, T,
U and V."

"Come on! Kill those spots!
Kill the mess!" yelled the cats.
And they jumped at the snow
With long rakes and red bats.
They put it in pails
And they made high pink hills!
Pink snow men! Pink snow balls!
And little pink pills!

Oh, the things that they did!
And they did them so hard,
It was all one big spot now
All over the yard!
But the Big Cat stood there
And he said, “This is good.
This is what they should do
And I knew that they would.

"With a little more help,
All the work will be done.
They need one more cat.
And I know just the one."

"Look close! In my hand
I have Little Cat V.
On his head are Cats W,
X, Y and Z."

"Z is too small to see.
So don't try. You can not.
But Z is the cat
Who will clean up that spot!"

“Now here is the Z
You can’t see,” said the Cat.
“And I bet you can’t guess
What he has in HIS hat!

“He has something called VOOM.
Voom is so hard to get,
You never saw anything
Like it, I bet.
Why, Voom cleans up anything
Clean as can be!”
Then he yelled,
“Take your hat off now,
Little Cat Z!
Take the Voom off your head!
Make it clean up the snow!
Hurry! You Little Cat!
One! Two! Three! GO!”

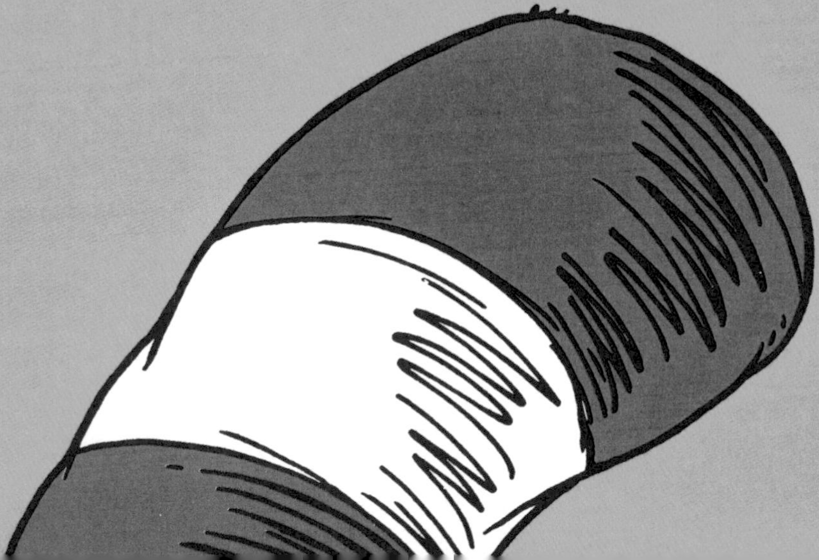

VOOM

Then the Voom . . .
It went VOOM!
And, oh boy! What a VOOM!

Now, don't ask me what Voom is.
I never will know.
But, boy! Let me tell you
It DOES clean up snow!

"So you see!" laughed the Cat,
"Now your snow is all white!
Now your work is all done!
Now your house is all right!
And you know where my little cats are?"
Said the cat.
"That Voom blew my little cats
Back in my hat.
And so, if you ever
Have spots, now and then,
I will be very happy
To come here again . . .

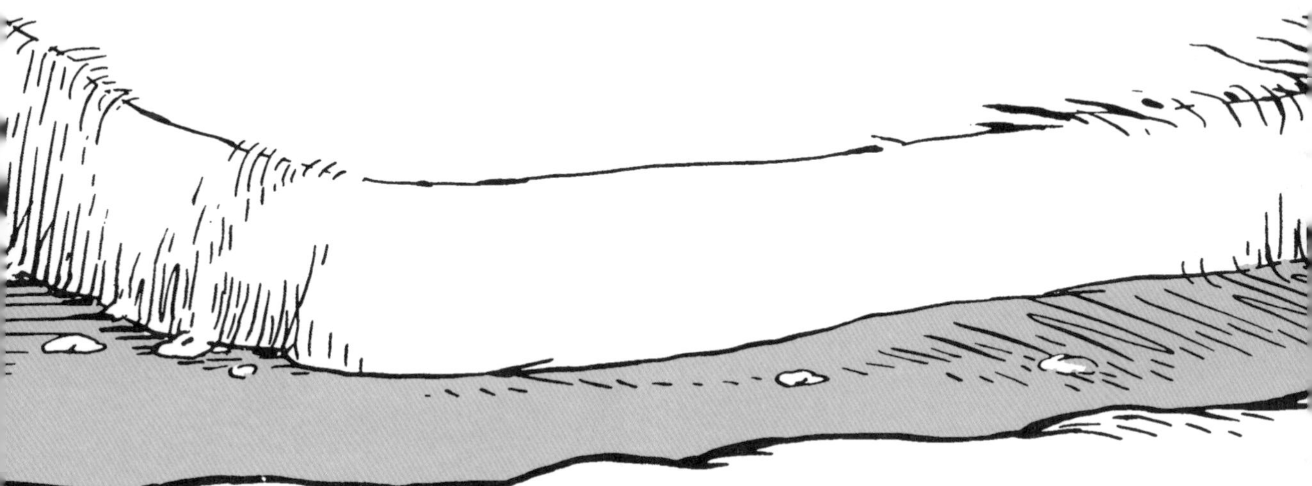

". . . with Little Cats A, B, C, D . . .

E, F, G . . .

H, I, J, K . . .

L, M, N . . .

and O, P . . .

and Q, R, S, T . . .

and Cat U and Cat V . . .

and Little Cats W

X

Y

and Z!"

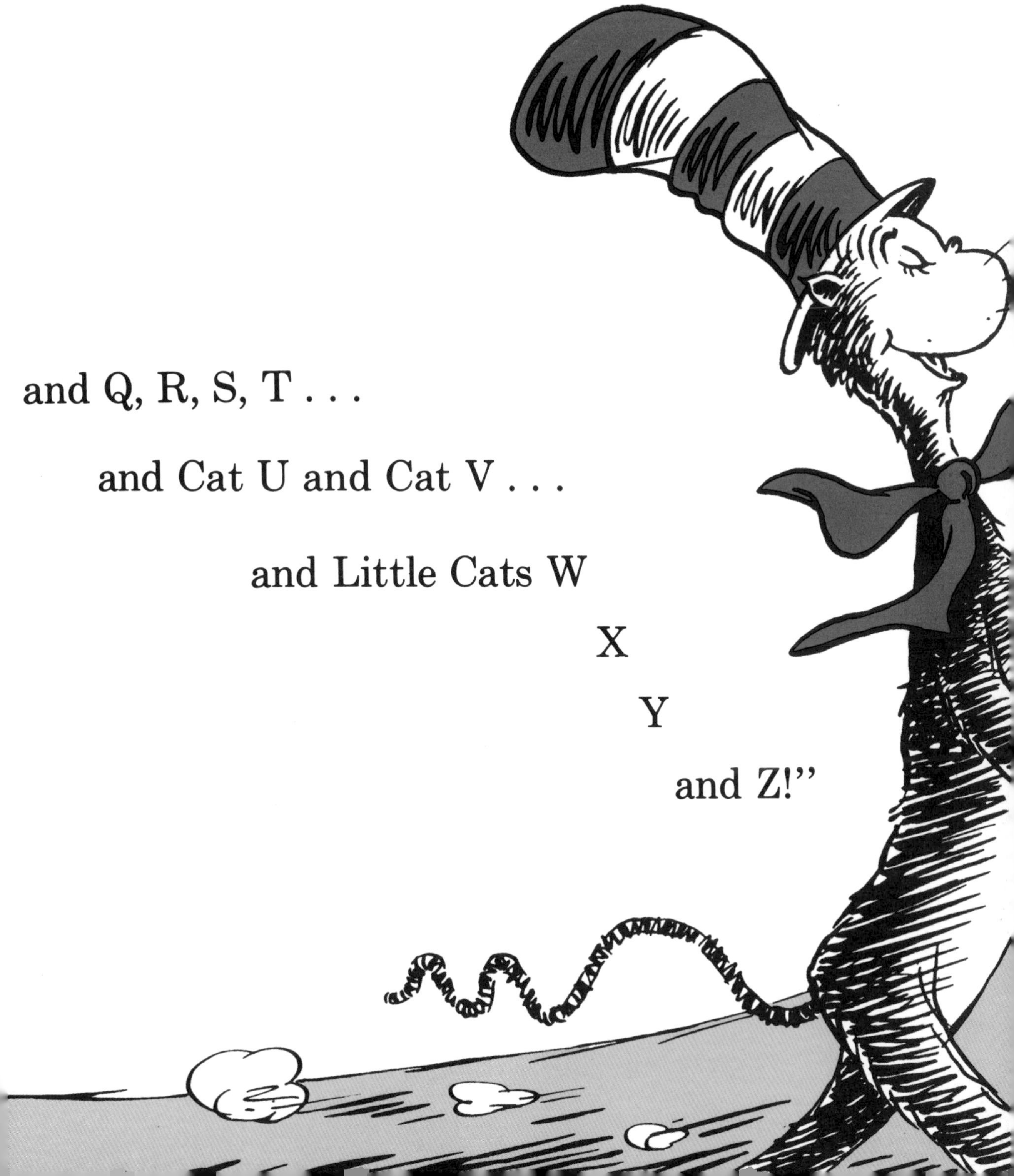

Green Eggs and Ham

I am Sam

I am Sam

Sam
I am

That Sam-I-am!

That Sam-I-am!

I do not like

that Sam-I-am!

Do you like

green eggs and ham?

I do not like them,
Sam-I-am.
I do not like
green eggs and ham.

Would you like them
here or there?

I would not like them
here or there.
I would not like them
anywhere.
I do not like
green eggs and ham.
I do not like them,
Sam-I-am.

Would you like them
in a house?
Would you like them
with a mouse?

I do not like them
in a house.
I do not like them
with a mouse.
I do not like them
here or there.
I do not like them
anywhere.
I do not like green eggs and ham.
I do not like them, Sam-I-am.

Would you eat them
in a box?
Would you eat them
with a fox?

Not in a box.

Not with a fox.

Not in a house.

Not with a mouse.

I would not eat them here or there.

I would not eat them anywhere.

I would not eat green eggs and ham.

I do not like them, Sam-I-am.

Would you? Could you?

In a car?

Eat them! Eat them!

Here they are.

I would not,
could not,
in a car.

You may like them.
You will see.
You may like them
in a tree!

I would not, could not in a tree.
Not in a car! You let me be.

I do not like them in a box.
I do not like them with a fox.
I do not like them in a house.
I do not like them with a mouse.
I do not like them here or there.
I do not like them anywhere.
I do not like green eggs and ham.
I do not like them, Sam-I-am.

A train! A train!
A train! A train!
Could you, would you,
on a train?

Not on a train! Not in a tree!
Not in a car! Sam! Let me be!

I would not, could not, in a box.
I could not, would not, with a fox.
I will not eat them with a mouse.
I will not eat them in a house.
I will not eat them here or there.
I will not eat them anywhere.
I do not eat green eggs and ham.
I do not like them, Sam-I-am.

Say!

In the dark?

Here in the dark!

Would you, could you, in the dark?

I would not, could not,

in the dark.

Would you, could you,
in the rain?

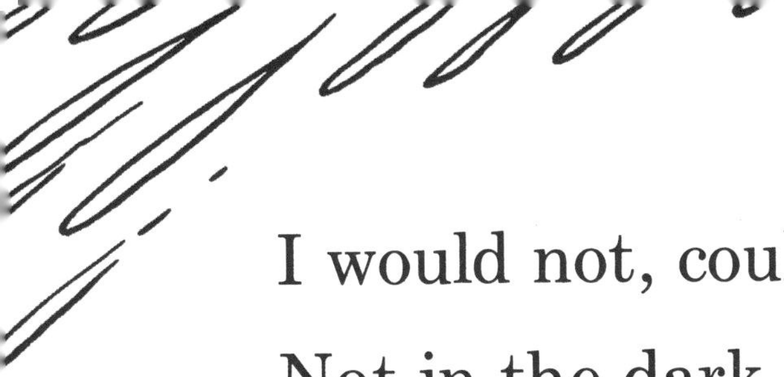

I would not, could not, in the rain.
Not in the dark. Not on a train.
Not in a car. Not in a tree.
I do not like them, Sam, you see.
Not in a house. Not in a box.
Not with a mouse. Not with a fox.
I will not eat them here or there.
I do not like them anywhere!

You do not like
green eggs and ham?

I do not
like them,
Sam-I-am.

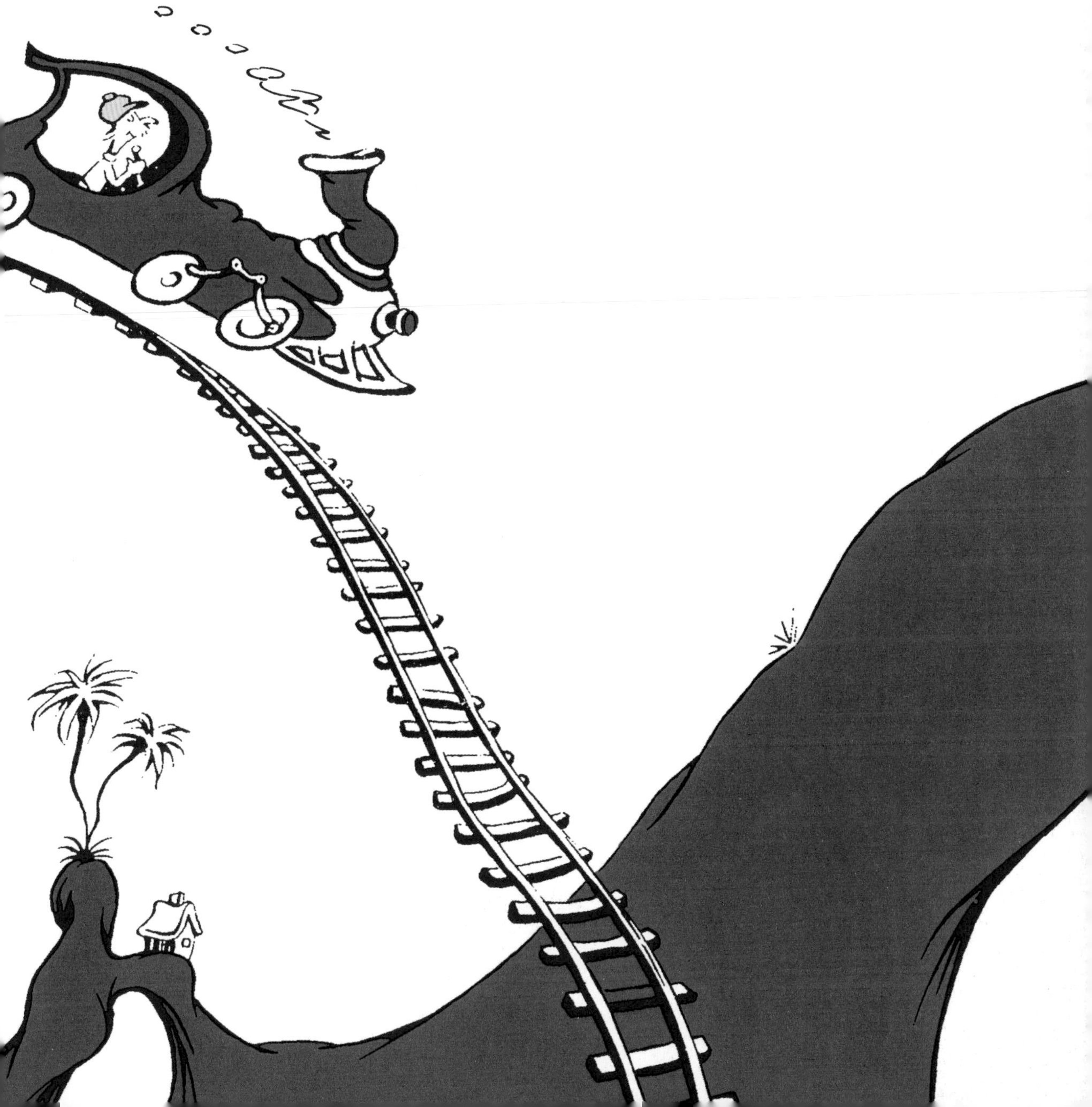

Could you, would you,
with a goat?

I would not,
could not,
with a goat!

Would you, could you,
on a boat?

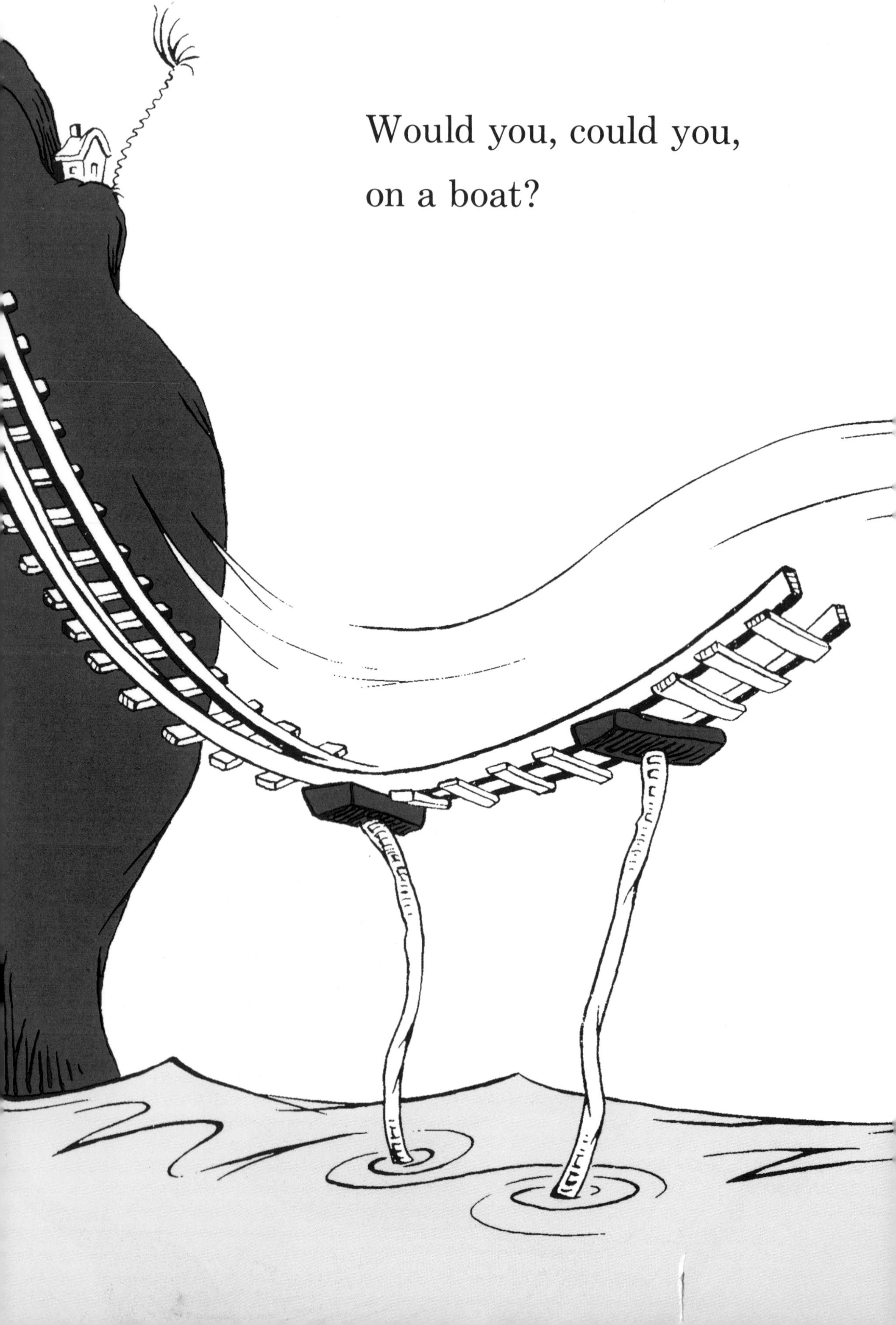

I could not, would not, on a boat.
I will not, will not, with a goat.
I will not eat them in the rain.
I will not eat them on a train.
Not in the dark! Not in a tree!
Not in a car! You let me be!
I do not like them in a box.
I do not like them with a fox.
I will not eat them in a house.
I do not like them with a mouse.
I do not like them here or there.
I do not like them ANYWHERE!

I do not like
green eggs
and ham!

I do not like them,

Sam-I-am.

You do not like them.

So you say.

Try them! Try them!

And you may.

Try them and you may, I say.

Sam!

If you will let me be,

I will try them.

You will see.

Sam!

I like green eggs and ham!

I do! I like them, Sam-I-am!

And I would eat them in a boat.

And I would eat them with a goat . . .

And I will eat them in the rain.
And in the dark. And on a train.
And in a car. And in a tree.
They are so good, so good, you see!

So I will eat them in a box.
And I will eat them with a fox.
And I will eat them in a house.
And I will eat them with a mouse.
And I will eat them here and there.
I will eat them ANYWHERE!

I do so like
green eggs and ham!
Thank you!
Thank you,
Sam-I-am!

Fox in Socks

Fox

Socks

Box

Knox

Knox in box.
Fox in socks.

Knox on fox
in socks in box.

Socks on Knox
and Knox in box.

Fox in socks
on box on Knox.

Chicks with bricks come.
Chicks with blocks come.
Chicks with bricks and
blocks and clocks come.

Look, sir. Look, sir.
Mr. Knox, sir.
Let's do tricks with
bricks and blocks, sir.
Let's do tricks with
chicks and clocks, sir.

First, I'll make a
quick trick brick stack.
Then I'll make a
quick trick block stack.

You can make a
quick trick chick stack.
You can make a
quick trick clock stack.

And here's a
new trick, Mr. Knox. . . .
Socks on chicks
and chicks on fox.
Fox on clocks
on bricks and blocks.
Bricks and blocks
on Knox on box.

Now we come to
ticks and tocks, sir.
Try to say this
Mr. Knox, sir. . . .

Clocks on fox tick.
Clocks on Knox tock.
Six sick bricks tick.
Six sick chicks tock.

Please, sir. I don't
like this trick, sir.
My tongue isn't
quick or slick, sir.
I get all those
ticks and clocks, sir,
mixed up with the
chicks and tocks, sir.
I can't do it, Mr. Fox, sir.

I'm so sorry,
Mr. Knox, sir.

Here's an easy
game to play.
Here's an easy
thing to say. . . .

New socks.
Two socks.
Whose socks?
Sue's socks.

Who sews whose socks?
Sue sews Sue's socks.

Who sees who sew
whose new socks, sir?
You see Sue sew
Sue's new socks, sir.

That's not easy,
Mr. Fox, sir.

Who comes? . . .
Crow comes.
Slow Joe Crow comes.

Who sews crow's clothes?
Sue sews crow's clothes.
Slow Joe Crow
sews whose clothes?
Sue's clothes.

Sue sews socks of
fox in socks now.

Slow Joe Crow sews
Knox in box now.

Sue sews rose
on Slow Joe Crow's clothes.
Fox sews hose
on Slow Joe Crow's nose.

Hose goes.
Rose grows.
Nose hose goes some.
Crow's rose grows some.

Mr. Fox!
I hate this game, sir.
This game makes
my tongue quite lame, sir.

Mr. Knox, sir,
what a shame, sir.

We'll find something
new to do now.
Here is lots of
new blue goo now.
New goo. Blue goo.
Gooey. Gooey.
Blue goo. New goo.
Gluey. Gluey.

Gooey goo
for chewy chewing!
That's what that
Goo-Goose is doing.
Do you choose to
chew goo, too, sir?
If, sir, you, sir,
choose to chew, sir,
with the Goo-Goose,
chew, sir. Do, sir.

Mr. Fox, sir,
I won't do it.
I can't say it.
I won't chew it.

Very well, sir.
Step this way.
We'll find another
game to play.

Bim comes.
Ben comes.
Bim brings Ben broom.
Ben brings Bim broom.

Ben bends Bim's broom.
Bim bends Ben's broom.
Bim's bends.
Ben's bends.
Ben's bent broom breaks.
Bim's bent broom breaks.

Ben's band. Bim's band.
Big bands. Pig bands.

Bim and Ben lead
bands with brooms.
Ben's band bangs
and Bim's band booms.

Pig band! Boom band!
Big band! Broom band!
My poor mouth can’t
say that. No, sir.
My poor mouth is
much too slow, sir.

Well then . . .
bring your mouth this way.
I'll find it something
it can say.

Luke Luck likes lakes.
Luke's duck likes lakes.
Luke Luck licks lakes.
Luke's duck licks lakes.

Duck takes licks
in lakes Luke Luck likes.
Luke Luck takes licks
in lakes duck likes.

I can't blab
such blibber blubber!
My tongue isn't
made of rubber.

Mr. Knox. Now
come now. Come now.
You don't have to
be so dumb now. . . .

Try to say this,
Mr. Knox, please. . . .

Through three cheese trees
three free fleas flew.
While these fleas flew,
freezy breeze blew.
Freezy breeze made
these three trees freeze.
Freezy trees made
these trees' cheese freeze.
That's what made these
three free fleas sneeze.

Stop it! Stop it!
That's enough, sir.
I can't say
such silly stuff, sir.

Very well, then,
Mr. Knox, sir.

Let's have a little talk
about tweetle beetles. . . .

What do you know
about tweetle beetles?
Well . . .

When tweetle beetles fight,
it's called
a tweetle beetle battle.

And when they
battle in a puddle,
it's a tweetle
beetle puddle battle.

AND when tweetle beetles
battle with paddles in a puddle,
they call it a tweetle
beetle puddle paddle battle.

AND . . .

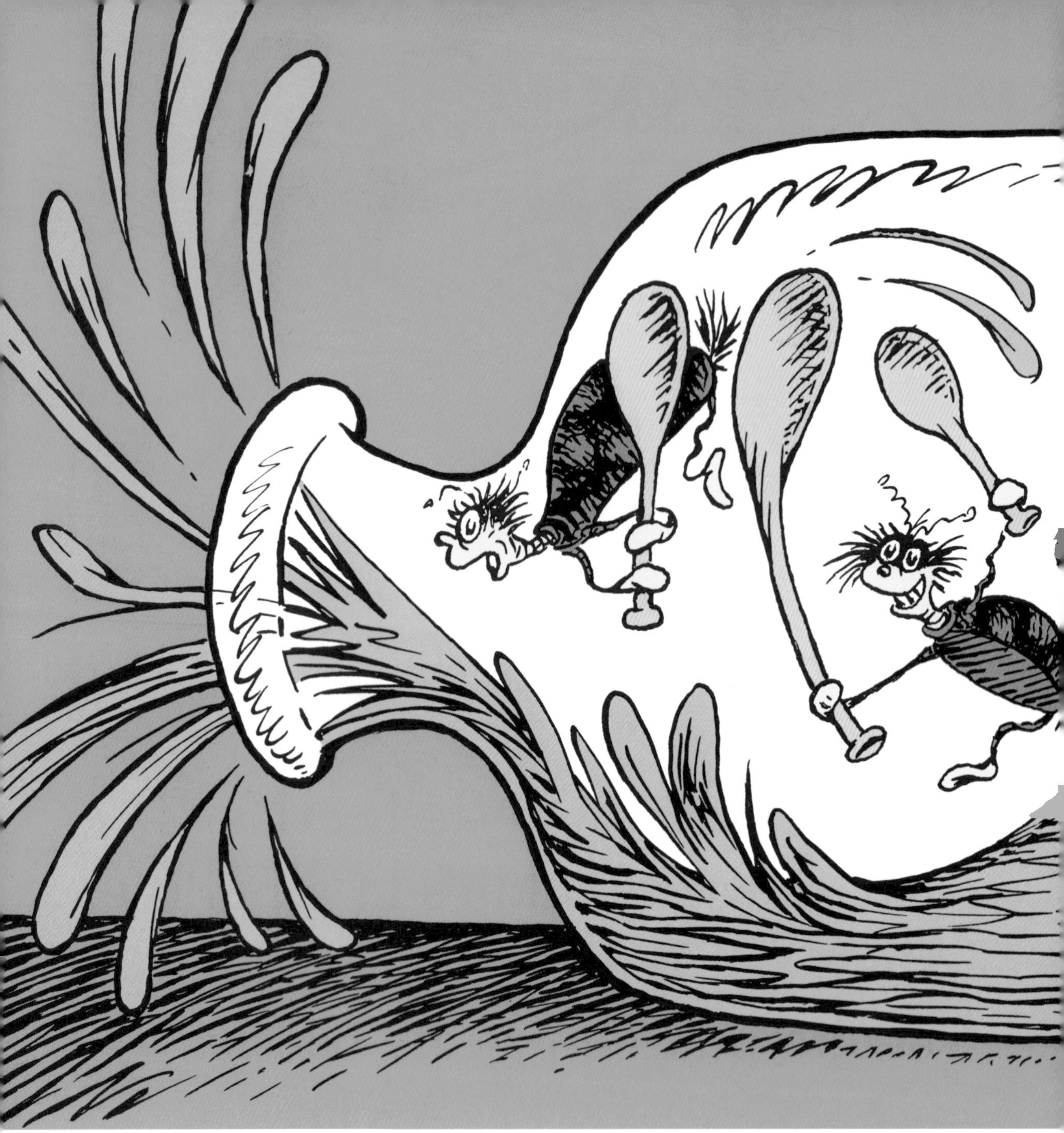

When beetles battle beetles
in a puddle paddle battle
and the beetle battle puddle
is a puddle in a bottle . . .

. . . they call this
a tweetle beetle
bottle puddle
paddle battle muddle.

AND . . .

When beetles
fight these battles
in a bottle
with their paddles
and the bottle's
on a poodle
and the poodle's
eating noodles . . .

. . . they call this
a muddle puddle
tweetle poodle
beetle noodle
bottle paddle battle.

AND . . .

Now wait
a minute,
Mr. Socks Fox!

When a fox is
in the bottle where
the tweetle beetles battle
with their paddles
in a puddle on a
noodle-eating poodle,
THIS is what they call . . .

. . . a tweetle beetle
noodle poodle bottled
paddled muddled duddled
fuddled wuddled
fox in socks, sir!

Fox in socks,
our game is done, sir.
Thank you for
a lot of fun, sir.

How The Grinch Stole Christmas!

By Dr. Seuss

Every *Who*
Down in *Who*-ville
Liked Christmas a lot . . .

But the Grinch,
Who lived just north of *Who*-ville,
Did NOT!

The Grinch *hated* Christmas! The whole Christmas season!
Now, please don't ask why. No one quite knows the reason.
It *could* be his head wasn't screwed on just right.
It *could* be, perhaps, that his shoes were too tight.
But I think that the most likely reason of all
May have been that his heart was two sizes too small.

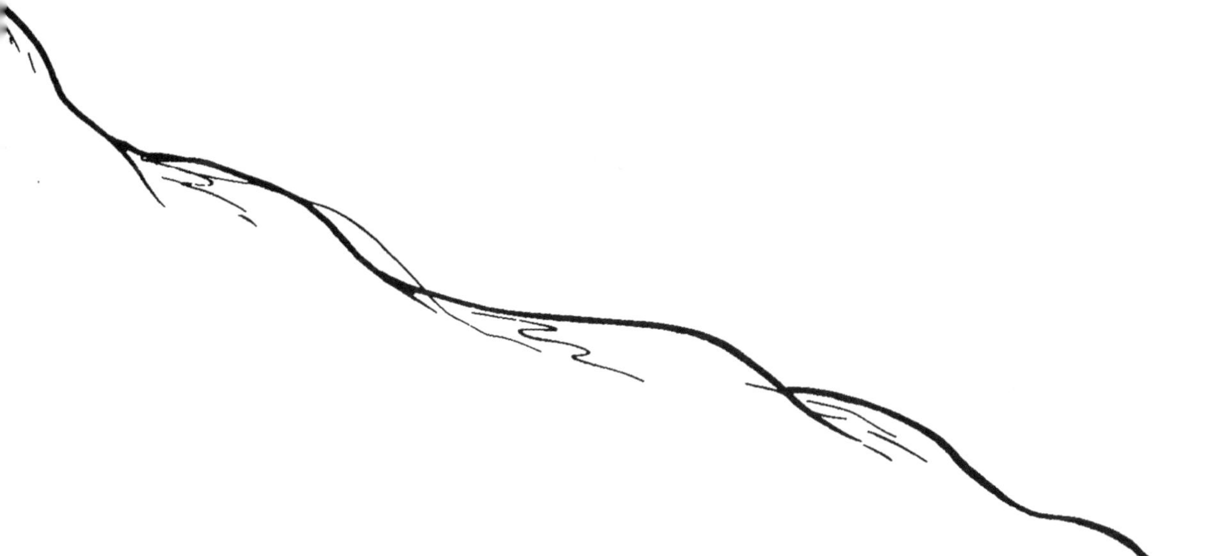

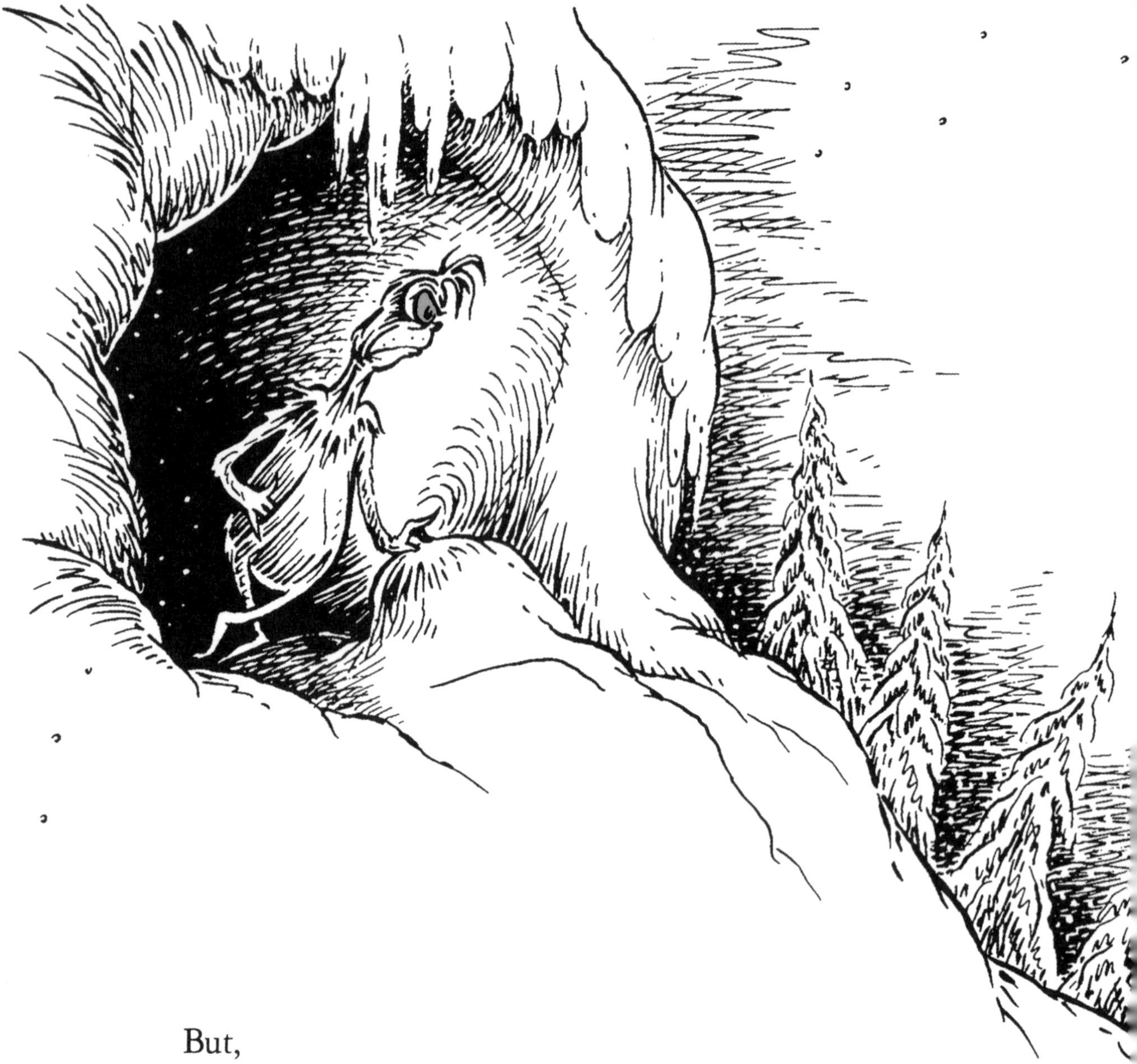

But,
Whatever the reason,
His heart or his shoes,
He stood there on Christmas Eve, hating the *Whos,*
Staring down from his cave with a sour, Grinchy frown
At the warm lighted windows below in their town.
For he knew every *Who* down in *Who*-ville beneath
Was busy now, hanging a mistletoe wreath.

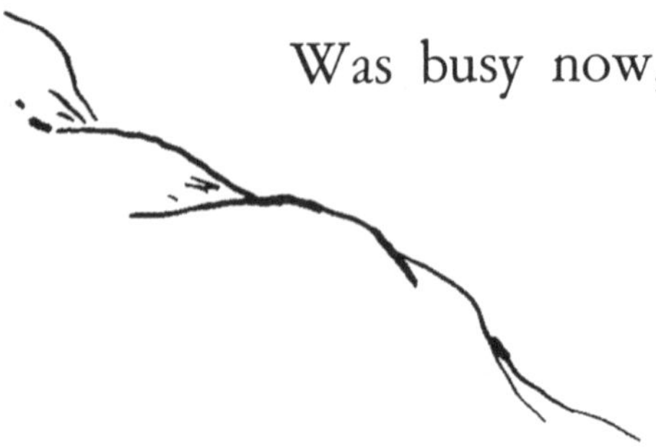

"And they're hanging their stockings!" he snarled with a sneer.
"Tomorrow is Christmas! It's practically here!"
Then he growled, with his Grinch fingers nervously drumming,
"I MUST find some way to stop Christmas from coming!"

For,
Tomorrow, he knew . . .

. . . All the *Who* girls and boys
Would wake bright and early. They'd rush for their toys!
And *then!* Oh, the noise! Oh, the Noise! Noise! Noise! Noise!
That's *one* thing he hated! The NOISE! NOISE! NOISE! NOISE!

Then the *Whos,* young and old, would sit down to a feast.
And they'd feast! *And they'd feast!*
And they'd FEAST!

FEAST!

FEAST!

FEAST!

They would feast on *Who*-pudding, and rare *Who*-roast-beast
Which was something the Grinch couldn't stand in the least!

MERRY
MERRY

And THEN
They'd do something
He liked least of all!
Every *Who* down in *Who*-ville, the tall and the small,
Would stand close together, with Christmas bells ringing.
They'd stand hand-in-hand. And the *Whos* would start singing!

They'd sing! *And they'd sing!*

AND they'd SING! SING! SING! SING!

And the more the Grinch thought of this *Who*-Christmas-Sing,
The more the Grinch thought, "I must stop this whole thing!
"Why, for fifty-three years I've put up with it now!
"I MUST stop this Christmas from coming!

. . . But HOW?"

Then he got an idea!

An awful idea!

THE GRINCH

GOT A WONDERFUL, AWFUL IDEA!

"I know *just* what to do!" The Grinch laughed in his throat.
And he made a quick Santa Claus hat and a coat.
And he chuckled, and clucked, "What a great Grinchy trick!
"With this coat and this hat, I look just like Saint Nick!"

"All I need is a reindeer . . ."
The Grinch looked around.
But, since reindeer are scarce, there was none to be found.
Did that stop the old Grinch . . . ?
No! The Grinch simply said,
"If I can't *find* a reindeer, I'll *make* one instead!"
So he called his dog, Max. Then he took some red thread
And he tied a big horn on the top of his head.

THEN
He loaded some bags
And some old empty sacks
On a ramshackle sleigh
And he hitched up old Max.

Then the Grinch said, "Giddap!"
And the sleigh started down
Toward the homes where the *Whos*
Lay a-snooze in their town.

All their windows were dark. Quiet snow filled the air.
All the *Whos* were all dreaming sweet dreams without care
When he came to the first little house on the square.
"This is stop number one," the old Grinchy Claus hissed
And he climbed to the roof, empty bags in his fist.

J.P.Who

MERRY CHRISTMAS
WHO Express
FOR JO-JO
FOR UNCLE WHO
FOR AUNTIE WHO

Then he slid down the chimney. A rather tight pinch.
But, if Santa could do it, then so could the Grinch.
He got stuck only once, for a moment or two.
Then he stuck his head out of the fireplace flue
Where the little *Who* stockings all hung in a row.
"These stockings," he grinned, "are the *first* things to go!"

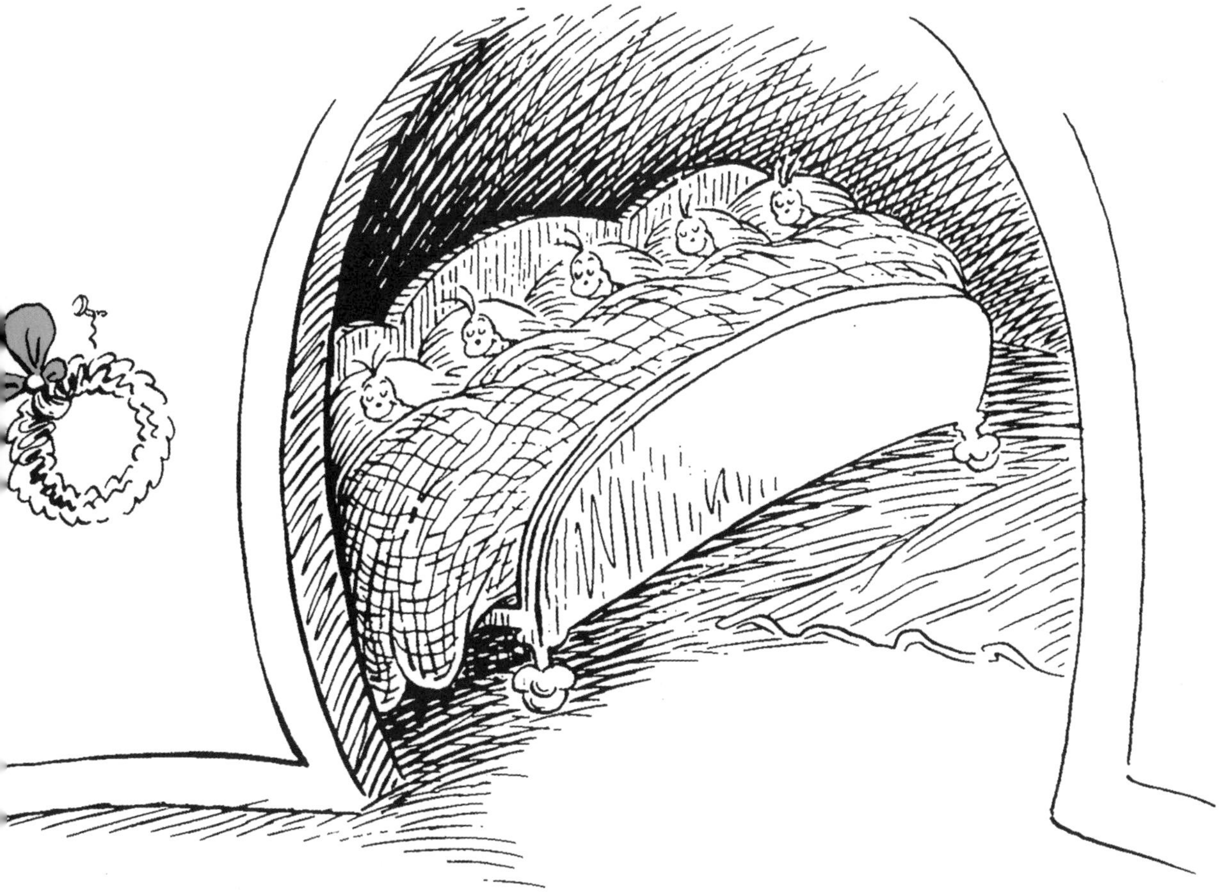

Then he slithered and slunk, with a smile most unpleasant,
Around the whole room, and he took every present!
Pop guns! And bicycles! Roller skates! Drums!
Checkerboards! Tricycles! Popcorn! And plums!
And he stuffed them in bags. Then the Grinch, very nimbly,
Stuffed all the bags, one by one, up the chimbley!

GENERAL
GW
WHO-LECTRIC

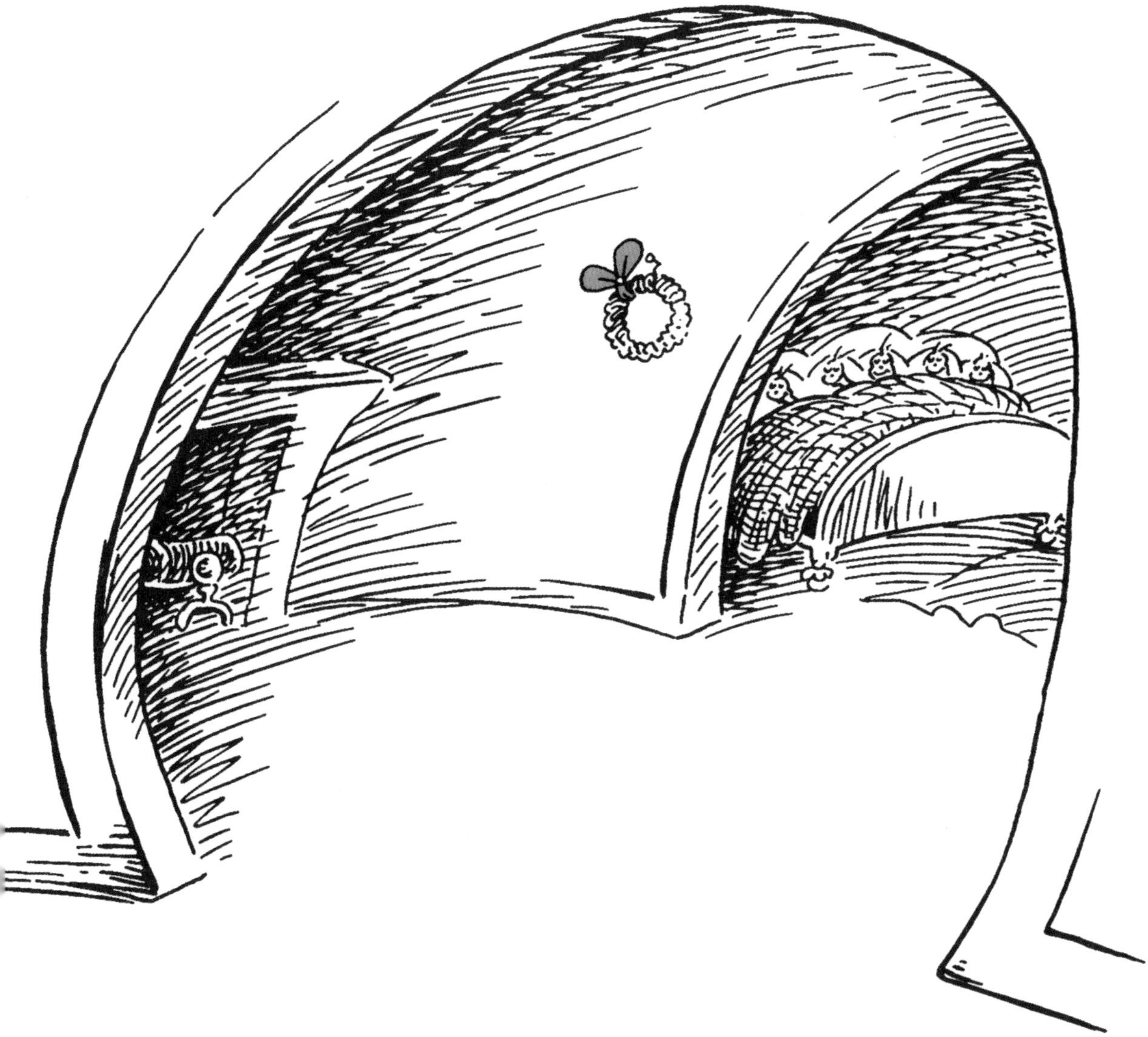

Then he slunk to the icebox. He took the *Whos'* feast!
He took the *Who*-pudding! He took the roast beast!
He cleaned out that icebox as quick as a flash.
Why, that Grinch even took their last can of *Who*-hash!

Then he stuffed all the food up the chimney with glee.
"And NOW!" grinned the Grinch, "I will stuff up the tree!"

And the Grinch grabbed the tree, and he started to shove
When he heard a small sound like the coo of a dove.
He turned around fast, and he saw a small *Who!*
Little Cindy-Lou *Who,* who was not more than two.

The Grinch had been caught by this tiny *Who* daughter
Who'd got out of bed for a cup of cold water.
She stared at the Grinch and said, "Santa Claus, why,
"*Why* are you taking our Christmas tree? WHY?"

But, you know, that old Grinch was so smart and so slick
He thought up a lie, and he thought it up quick!
"Why, my sweet little tot," the fake Santa Claus lied,
"There's a light on this tree that won't light on one side.
"So I'm taking it home to my workshop, my dear.
"I'll fix it up *there.* Then I'll bring it back *here.*"

And his fib fooled the child. Then he patted her head
And he got her a drink and he sent her to bed.
And when Cindy-Lou *Who* went to bed with her cup,
HE went to the chimney and stuffed the tree up!

Then the *last* thing he took
Was the log for their fire!
Then he went up the chimney, himself, the old liar.
On their walls he left nothing but hooks and some wire.

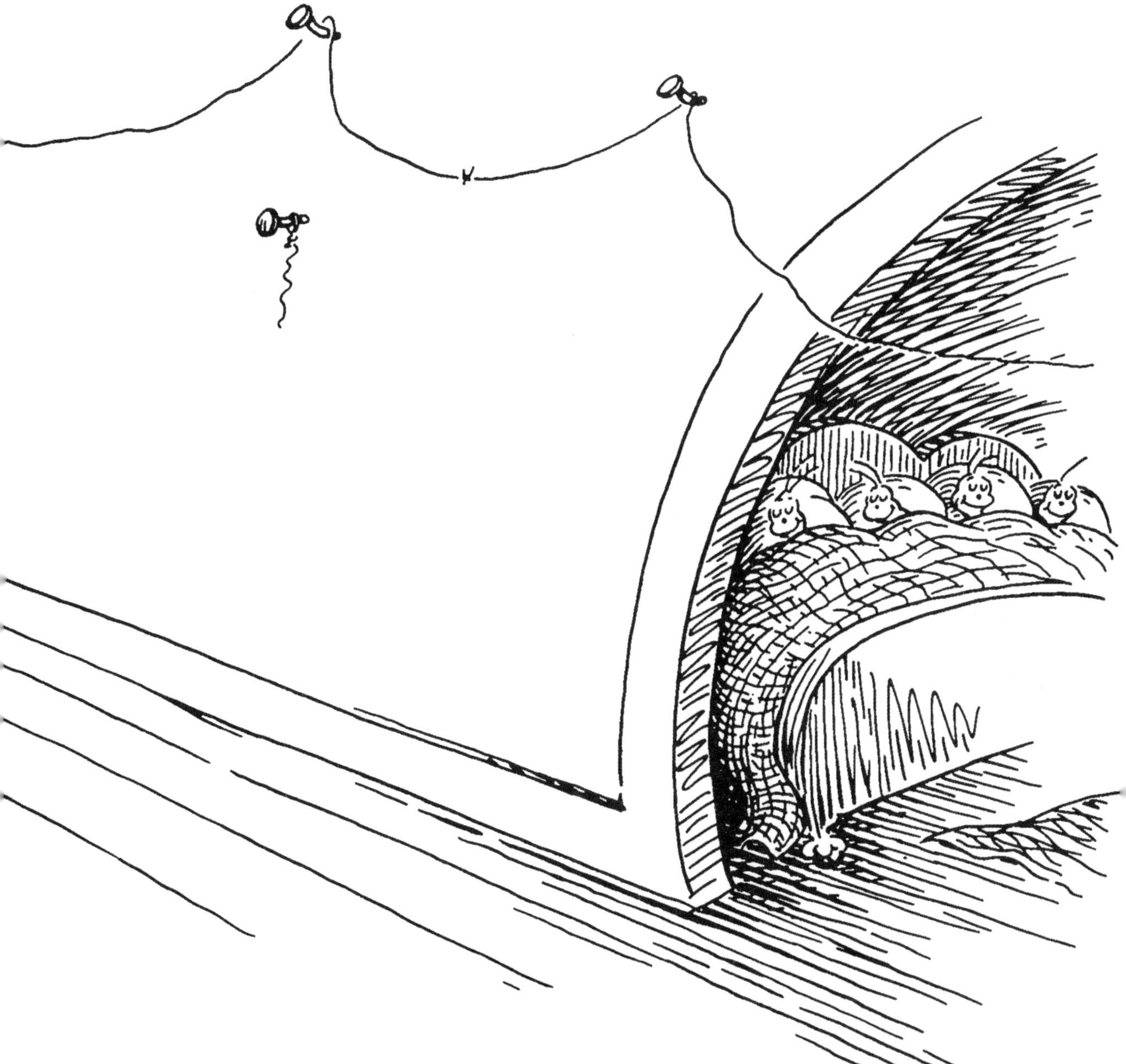

And the one speck of food
That he left in the house
Was a crumb that was even too small for a mouse.

Then

He did the *same* thing
To the *other Whos'* houses

Leaving crumbs
Much too small
For the other *Whos'* mouses!

MERRY MERRY

It was quarter past dawn . . .
All the *Whos,* still a-bed,
All the *Whos,* still a-snooze
When he packed up his sled,
Packed it up with their presents! The ribbons! The wrappings!
The tags! And the tinsel! The trimmings! The trappings!

Three thousand feet up! Up the side of Mt. Crumpit,
He rode with his load to the tiptop to dump it!
"Pooh-Pooh to the *Whos!*" he was grinch-ish-ly humming.
"They're finding out now that no Christmas is coming!
"They're just waking up! I know *just* what they'll do!
"Their mouths will hang open a minute or two
"Then the *Whos* down in *Who*-ville will all cry BOO-HOO!

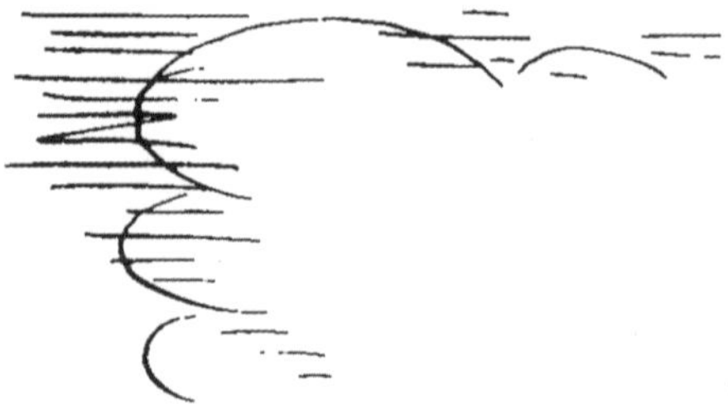

"That's a noise," grinned the Grinch,
"That I simply MUST hear!"
So he paused. And the Grinch put his hand to his ear.
And he *did* hear a sound rising over the snow.
It started in low. Then it started to grow . . .

But the sound wasn't *sad!*
Why, this sound sounded *merry!*
It *couldn't* be so!
But it WAS merry! VERY!

He stared down at *Who*-ville!
The Grinch popped his eyes!
Then he shook!
What he saw was a shocking surprise!

Every *Who* down in *Who*-ville, the tall and the small,
Was singing! Without any presents at all!

He HADN'T stopped Christmas from coming!

IT CAME!

Somehow or other, it came just the same!

And the Grinch, with his grinch-feet ice-cold in the snow,
Stood puzzling and puzzling: "How *could* it be so?
"It came without ribbons! It came without tags!
"It came without packages, boxes or bags!"
And he puzzled three hours, till his puzzler was sore.
Then the Grinch thought of something he hadn't before!
"Maybe Christmas," he thought, "*doesn't* come from a store.
"Maybe Christmas . . . perhaps . . . means a little bit more!"

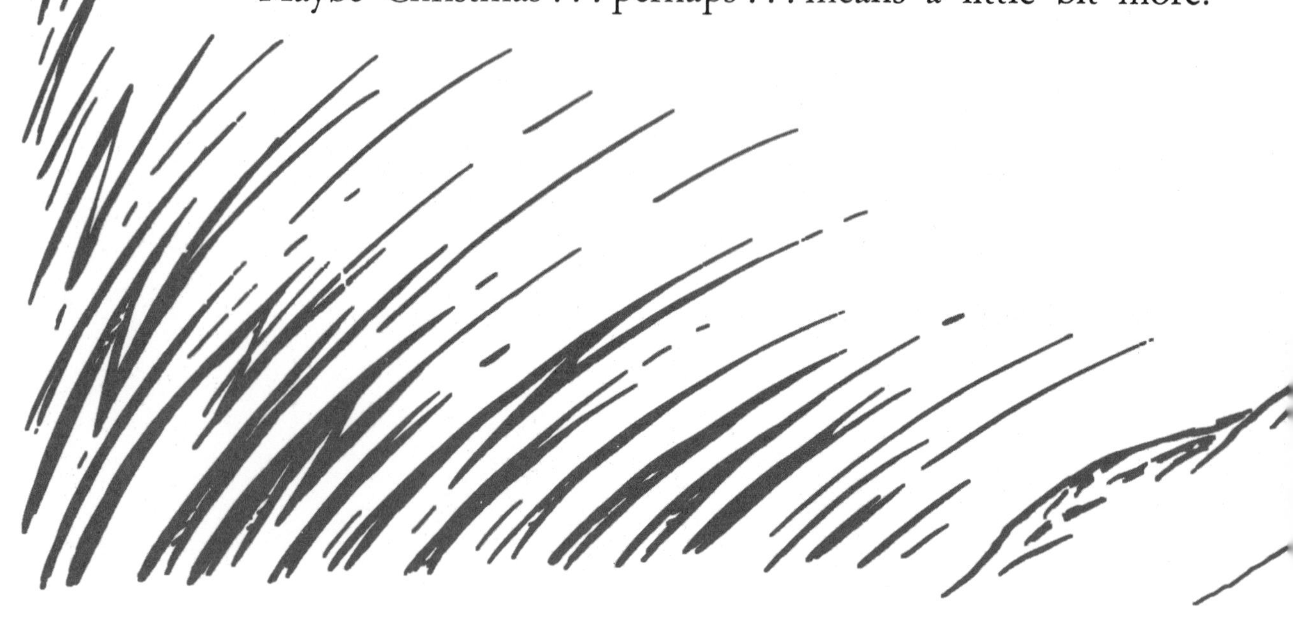

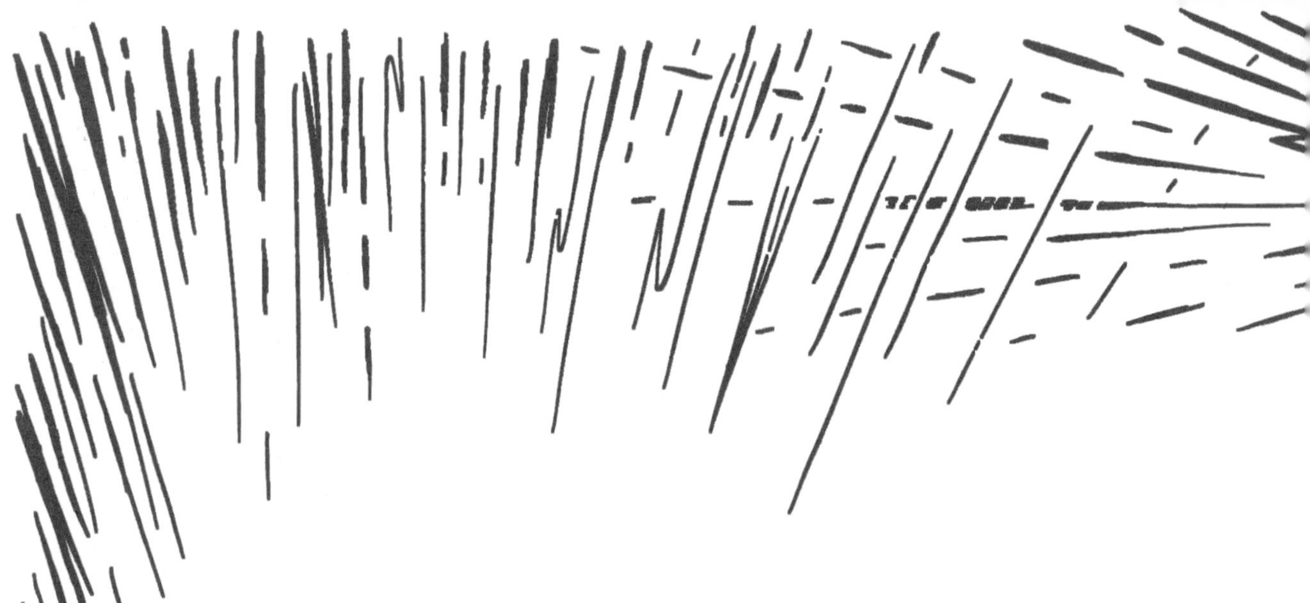

And what happened *then* . . . ?
Well . . . in *Who*-ville they say
That the Grinch's small heart
Grew three sizes that day!
And the minute his heart didn't feel quite so tight,
He whizzed with his load through the bright morning light
And he brought back the toys! And the food for the feast!
And he . . .

. . . HE HIMSELF . . . !

The Grinch carved the roast beast!